KAREN WALLACE
Scarlette Beane

Illustrated by JON BERKELEY

OXFORD
UNIVERSITY PRESS

When Mrs Beane first saw her daughter's face, it was red as a beetroot and the ends of her fingers were green.

'I shall call
her Scarlette,'
declared
Mrs Beane.
'She will grow
tall and strong
and do something
wonderful.'

Mr and Mrs Beane lived in
a house that looked like a
garden shed.

It was cosy and made of
wood but it was very small.

So they worked outside
as much as they could.

Scarlette lay in her pram and listened to the flowers grow.

And when she slept, she dreamed of doing something wonderful.

On her fifth birthday, Grandfather Beane
gave Scarlette a vegetable garden.

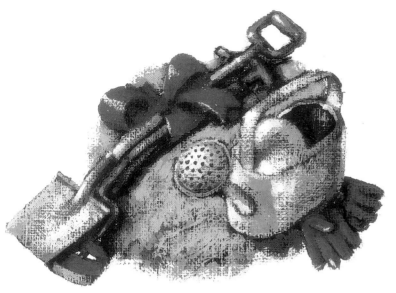

Her mother gave her a set of tools with wooden handles.

Her father built a wooden fence to keep out the rabbits.

And he made a white gate Scarlette could open herself.

Scarlette loved her new garden.
She pulled up the weeds.

She dug the soil until it was
crumbly like chocolate cake.

She planted a row of
carrots, a row of onions,
and a row of parsley.

That night when she went to bed, the ends
of her fingers glowed like green lights.

The next morning Scarlette ran to her garden.

Her carrots were huge
as tree trunks.

Her onions were as big
as hot air balloons.

Her parsley was as thick
as a jungle.

Everyone in the village came to help.

They used bulldozers to dig the carrots.

They drove forklift trucks
to carry the onions.

They cut the parsley
with chain saws.

Mrs Beane's kitchen was too small for so many vegetables. So she made soup in a concrete mixer.

The house was too small for so many people.

So Mr Beane served the
soup in the garden.
Everyone said it was the
best soup ever.

And when it began to
rain they ate second
helpings under the table.

That night Scarlette Beane
dreamed of something wonderful.

She crept out of bed. In one hand
she held a small trowel. In the other,
she had lots and lots of seeds.

High above the meadow,
the moon hung like a pearl
in the sky.

Scarlette dug a hole and put
all the seeds at the bottom.

As she covered them with
earth, the ends of her fingers
flashed like green stars.

The next morning the sun rose like
a huge gold coin. In the middle of the
meadow was a castle made of vegetables.

It had turnip turrets.
And a drawbridge held
up by corn cobs.

A cucumber tower
stood at each corner.

Mr Beane couldn't believe his eyes.
It was the house of all his dreams.

Mrs Beane kissed her
daughter's face.

'I knew you'd do
something wonderful,'
she whispered.

Scarlette Beane was
so happy, she went
red as a beetroot.

And the ends of
her fingers sparkled
like fireworks.

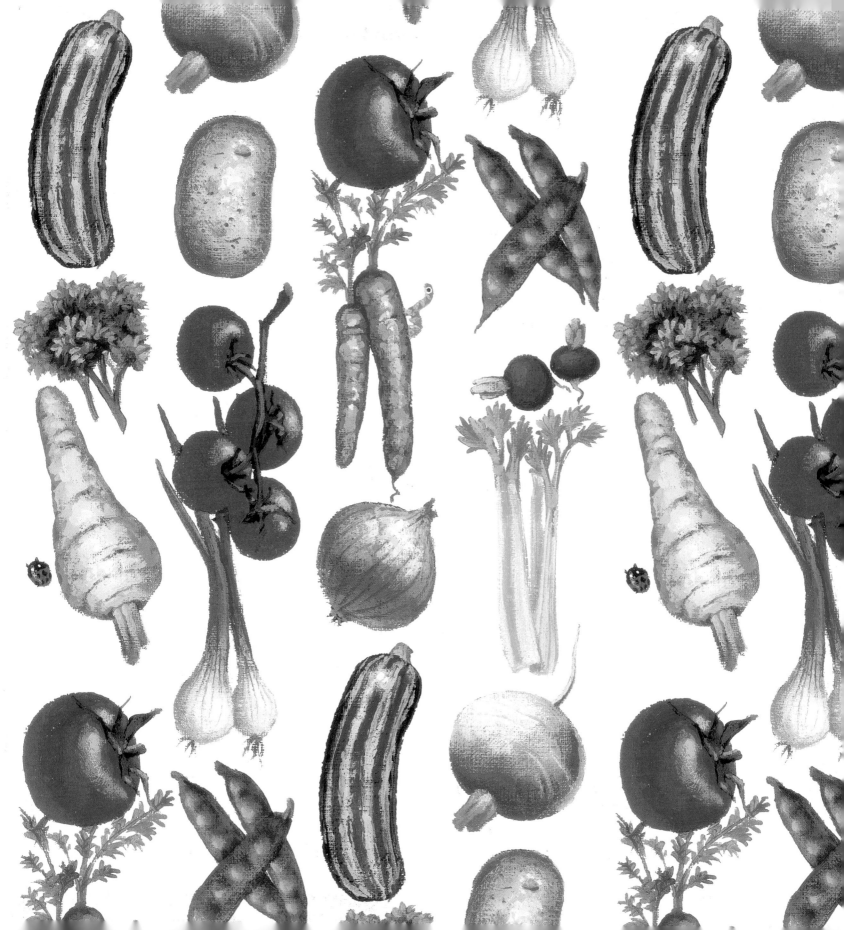